DEDICATION

To the innerchild in all of us who is in love with everything and everyone .

PREFACE

A trip where we all go separately . The place is always the same , but emotions and journey are different .

On a trip I realized the true meaning of love . We never understand love until we break our heart . Each broken part of us is radiating the shine that we hold in love for everyone in our life . The memories of those emotions till date that have been passed through my mind are reaching out to the core of my memory . I had share those moments through this writing .

ACKNOWLEDGEMENT

I m thankful to ;

My dad Mr Ashwani Kumar for the love and all the lessons and support ,

My mum Mrs Mona Chaudhary for the inspiration ,

My mentors Deepak Chaudhary and Rakesh Singh for guiding the way,

And to everyone who ever said anything positive to me .

TABLE OF CONTENT

1.

That day ,

When you held my hand ,

I realised that ,

Even my hands doesn't deserve you ,

Even they didn't fit in together ;

Then ,

How I could had a chance ,

To be in your life forever ,

So this moments are precious ,

And holding them is heaven ,

They would leave one day with sever injuries ;

Still I want to hold them to get ,

Those   scars   as   my   jewelleries   .

2.

Let's move in the woods ,

Let's build in the hoods ,

We are the Mavericks lost in mountains ,

And   our   sanity   got   hooked   .

3.

Always on my mind ,

Forever in my eyes ,

Mirror cant describe ;

The beauty I saw inside ,

Magical charm sprinkle ;

Upon me ,

Insanely I lost in the universe ;

Those eyes hold ,

My sense know way to ;

The world we belong ,

Now barely I remember ;

The   way   back   to   home   .

4.

You are my honey ,

Dripping that love potion ,

The way I crave for you ,

It's so magical to view ,

Like a bee ,

I m gravitated towards you ,

Even if you stung ,

I   m   gonna   stick   with   you   .

5.

On a cold night ,

You held my hand ,

And whispered ;

Let's travel to chill our bone ,

Vast wild ,

Will scare the evil inside ,

Trilling the song ,

" Ooh Moonchild ;

Things gonna be wild ,

Just hold tight ,

We gonna be high ,

Night is still ,

Young   and   wild   "   .

6.

Place's are common ,

Until ,

Moments are instil ,

That's when it flourish ,

In heavenward ;

Where feelings are ,

Prancing   upon   .

7.

One day we meet ,

And ,

My heart got intertwine with your's ,

My soul got knitted with your's ,

That's when I was done seeking ,

I found the ember ,

I searched ,

For million forevers ,

I fell for you long ago before beginnings .

8.

At time I feel this moment get seized ,

We got closed in the coolness of wind ,

Wrapped in starry blanket ,

Moon just winked ,

Surrounding got filled with love essence ,

As we were lost in one another ,

Blossoming   that   magical   aura   .

9.

Cafe's have witness ,

Many hearts calming close ,

Love brewing with ;

Glance , small talk ,

Just a cup ,

So , many stories it told ,

Our's was a fairytale ,

That   it   wrote   .

10.

Today ,

I wore diamond earrings ,

But my ears got hurt ,

Red and hot they turn ,

So , I wore the spiral galaxy ,

That you bought ,

Soon discomfort went off ,

Your instilled love healed them ,

We have been excited ,

About such a great deal ,

Just in pennies ;

galaxy ,

You   bought   .

11.

He came and I realised ,

The worth of my life .

He held my hand and ,

I found the lost sunshine .

Hope was blown to my lungs ,

By his tongue .

Touch's brought ashes to life .

Phoenix raise through his eyes .

Fire burnt the hell inside .

Bloom   the   heaven   of   desires   .

12.

As I remember that evening walk ,

I felt like our chit chat like ;

Reciting poetry to you ,

Your whitening smile felt true ,

All of sudden dopamine run through ,

Your company was the sweet wine ,

I   crave   for   more   .

13.

We saw mountains ,

Twirling around moon ,

We watched stars ,

Sprinkling stardust ,

Ganga sang the lullaby ,

And stillness of night ,

Inherently cured our wounds ,

Nature have secrets to ,

Treat   illness   cities   caused   .

14.

This ,

Photographs revoke ,

All those memories ,

All that we experienced ;

Can't be brought ,

Now we have stories to paint on ,

This journey was the art ,

And   infinity   was   the   cost   .

15.

He is the sun ,

Bounded with the sky in her .

He is the magic ,

Of her wand .

He is the fire ,

Of her flames .

He is the water ,

Of her tides .

He is the nature ,

Of her earth .

He is the moon ,

Of her stars .

He lure the ;

Universe in her ,

With the burning ;

Glow   of   their   amour   .

16.

You took my heart for the ;

Very first time we collide   ,

My eyes confessed the love on our glance ,

My senses banged my hearts wall ;

The moment you hold ,

You were the one I waited so long ,

I was yours before I knew ,

Now I know the heart racing,   glancing and the way ;

I stumble upon you ,

First love has a meaning only known by you .

17.

O love ,

Meet me ;

In the end ,

When everything gonna ,

Be alright ,

You don't have to fight ,

Where world gonna ,

Be bright ,

I can hold you tight ,

Where sun gonna rise ,

Moon would shine ,

Where river gonna ,

Met the horizon ,

Where you by my side ,

Nothing to fright ,

Stars fall to wish upon ,

A world ,

Where love is lord ,

Intone the prayer ,

That   hit   every   soul   .

18.

I saw you and felt butterflies ,

Is this teenage love ?

You smiled my heart skipped a beat ,

Is this teenage love ?

You brought sunshine to my darkness ,

Is this teenage love ?

Your eyes shine like sapphire bringing ,

That fire to me ,

Your voice bring nightingale melody to me ,

Is this teenage love ?

Your philosophy silvering upon my world ,

Is this teenage love ?

The Roses I expected were never brought ,

But your fragrance encircling me ,

Like a honeybee and I felt like a rose ;

You have enchanted your moonshine upon me ;

And I wouldn't be cured by this charm ,

Is   this   our   kind   of   teenage   love   ?

19.

In every walk with you ,

I received more than ,

I was seeking ,

You were the hidden treasure ,

I found on this peak ,

Was digging for gold ,

But   got   a   gem   .

20.

As we meet these yogi's ,

We got to know ,

There was something divine ,

There was something to unwind ,

There was something to vibe ,

That open our eyes ,

The world which we inherit ,

Has something to uncover ,

Something to evolve ,

Something to learn that's going to ,

Teach us on which ,

We all will live ,

Upon .